Walt Disney's
MICKEY MOUSE
Those Were the Days

By Mary Carey
Illustrated by Mones

A GOLDEN BOOK • NEW YORK
Western Publishing Company, Inc., Racine, Wisconsin 53404

"Hurry, Uncle Mickey, we're late!" cried Morty.

"We're not late," said Mickey. "The sun isn't even up yet."

"But Mr. Bumbles is up," said Ferdie.

He pointed to a sign that read "Founders' Village," a landmark that showed what life was like in the olden days. There stood Mr. Bumbles, the caretaker, with his suitcase and his train ticket. He was all ready to leave on his vacation.

Morty and Ferdie ran to say good-bye to Mr. Bumbles. Mickey and the boys were to be the caretakers of Founders' Village while Mr. Bumbles was away.

"We know just what to do!" said Morty. "Every morning the horse gets hitched to the surrey. Then when all the people come, we'll take them for a surrey ride around the village."

"Afterward we'll serve homemade lemonade and popcorn," Ferdie said. "We'll make the popcorn on the wood-burning stove."

"Sounds like you have it down pat," said Mr. Bumbles.

A taxi came up the hill, and Mr. Bumbles got in and sped away.

"Won't this be fun!" cried Ferdie. "A whole week living just the way our grandparents did."

"Those were the days, huh?" Morty chuckled as they started for the stable to hitch up the horse.

The horse had other ideas. It would not go near the
surrey, and it would not stand still. The horse pranced and
stamped and reared. The boys scampered and prodded and
pleaded, but they could not get the harness on the animal.

Mickey tried to help the boys. The horse made a snorting, whinnying noise at him. Then it trotted into the stable and wouldn't come out again.

Morty sighed. "Maybe nobody will want a surrey ride today," he said. "Maybe if we give people lots of lemonade and popcorn, they won't even remember we have a surrey."

"We can hope," said Mickey, but he didn't sound too hopeful.

Mickey and the boys went to the kitchen to start on the lemonade. Instead of a faucet, they found a pump for water. Mickey pumped the handle up and down, up and down. The pump rattled and squealed and squeaked, but not a drop of water came out.

Morty searched the cupboards. "Where's the juicer?" he cried. "And where's the outlet to plug in the juicer? We can't squeeze lemons without a juicer."

"We can't serve lemonade without ice, either," said Ferdie. "There are no ice cubes in this refrigerator."

"It's not a refrigerator," said Mickey. "It's an icebox, and it's empty.

"I'll go to town later and buy some ice," said Mickey.

"Could you buy some wood, too?" asked Morty. "The woodbox is empty."

"There's a woodpile behind the stable," said Mickey. "You know what that means?"

"Does it mean we're supposed to chop big pieces of wood into little pieces?" asked Ferdie.

Mickey grinned. "You're living in the good old days now, and in those days boys chopped wood."

The boys sighed, but they chopped the wood. Then
Mickey made a fire in the old stove.
For about three minutes the small fire burned brightly.

Then smoke began to billow out into the kitchen.

"Uncle Mickey, the stove's on fire!" yelled Morty.

Mickey opened the stove lid. "Water!" he shouted. "Get water! I'll put it out!"

But there was no water. The pump didn't work.

Ferdie coughed and choked. He pulled the front door open. "I'll call the fire department!" he yelled.

He ran around Founders' Village, looking for a telephone, but there was none to be found. In the good old days people didn't have telephones.

By the time Ferdie got back to the house, the fire had died down. Mickey had thrown baking soda on the fire to put it out.

"That does it," said Mickey. "You two air out the kitchen. I'm going to town."

Mickey drove away toward town. When he came back, he had ice for the ice box.

"I made a couple of phone calls in town," Mickey told the boys. "Help is on the way."

Before long there was a rattling, clanking, chugging, puffing sound on the road. It was Goofy speeding to the rescue in his old car.

Minnie Mouse was with Goofy. So were Horace Horsecollar and Clarabelle Cow.

Clarabelle had once lived in the country, so she knew about wood-burning stoves. She turned a handle on the stovepipe. "That opens the draft," she said. "Now the stovepipe is clear and the smoke can go up the chimney."

Sure enough, when Mickey started a new fire in the stove, not a puff of smoke came out into the kitchen. Clarabelle started popping corn.

Minnie had never lived in the country, but she knew that lemonade was invented before people knew about electricity. She opened a cupboard and took out a funny-looking gadget.

"My grandma had a hand juicer, and it worked just fine," Minnie said. "This one should work, too. Ferdie, cut some lemons."

Ferdie did, and Minnie squeezed them on the hand juicer.

Horace Horsecollar fiddled with the pump. "I don't think it's broken," he said. "It just needs to be primed with water. It's a lucky thing I brought some water, just in case."

Horace carried a pail in from the car. He poured water from the pail into the pump. Then he moved the pump handle up and down.

This time the pump did not make an empty, rattling, squeaking sound. This time the pump gushed water.

"Great!" cried Ferdie. "Now we'll be all set if somebody can figure out an easy way to chop some more wood."

"No problem," said Horace. He led Morty and Ferdie out to the woodpile.

A car was pulling into a parking spot near the stable. A mother and father were in the front seat of the car, and two kids were in the backseat.

"Start chopping," Horace told the boys. "And smile! You love to chop wood! You're having a great time!"

"You've got to be kidding!" said Morty. But he and Ferdie began to chop the wood with huge grins on their faces. They even laughed out loud now and then as they worked.

The kids from the car wandered over to see what was happening. After they watched for a minute, one of them said, "Hey, Dad, can I chop some wood?"

"You can if you promise to be very careful," said the father. "I'll stand here and watch."

"Oh, maybe you'd better not," said Morty.

"It's really hard work," added Ferdie.

But the kids begged and pleaded. Soon Morty and Ferdie gave up their axes and let the visitors chop the wood.

"Pretty smart, aren't you?" said Morty to Horace. "Maybe you know how we can hitch the horse to the surrey."

But Goofy was tending to the horse. He led the horse out of the stable, and he whispered something in the horse's ear.

The horse gave a startled snort. Then it backed up to the surrey and stood still, and Goofy hitched it up.

Presto! The surrey was ready for a load of passengers.
"What did you say to the horse?" gasped Ferdie.

"I told him if he wanted to lose his job, I could fix it
for him," said Goofy. "I said that my jalopy is as old as
anything in Founders' Village, but it will start easier than a
stubborn horse, and people love to ride in it."

The rest of the day was grand.

The rest of the week was even better, with surrey rides and fresh lemonade and hot popcorn for everyone.

"The olden days really were good, weren't they?" said Ferdie.

"You bet," said Mickey. "But with good friends, any day is good."